COUNTDOWN TO KINDERGARTEN

by

Alison McGhee

Pictures by

Harry Bliss

SCHOLASTIC INC.

New York Toronto London Auckland Sydney
Mexico City New Delhi Hong Kong Buenos Aires

ISBN 0-439-78427-1

12 11 10 9 8 7 6 5 4 3 2 1   5 6 7 8 9 10/0

Printed in the U.S.A.   40

First Scholastic printing, September 2005

The pictures in this book were done in black ink
and watercolor on Arches 90 lb. watercolor paper.
The display lettering was created by Harry Bliss.
The text type was hand lettered by Paul Colin.
Designed by Suzanne Fridley

For Devon O'Brien
—A. M.

For Carol Dolnick
—H. B.

Rule #3: You're not allowed to bring any stuffed animals.

Rule #2: You're not allowed to bring your cat.

Rule #1: You have to know how to tie your shoes. By yourself. You're not allowed to ask for help. Ever.

NINE DAYS BEFORE KINDERGARTEN.

This isn't getting any easier.

LATER...

Mom finds everything.

Even the rain puddle is out to get me.

I know…I'll pull the laces out. Imagine what could happen if I left them in…

I know…I'll throw them out.

Dad says a lot of five-year-olds don't know how to tie.
I guess he hasn't heard Kindergarten Rule #1.

Dad practices with me.

Bunny ears, bunny ears, cross through.

Look at his knot. Just the way he showed me.

Puddy, here's your lunch.

LATER THAT DAY...

Repeat after me: Bowls are for cat food, shoes are for your feet.

Mom says a lot of five-year-olds don't know how to tie.
I guess *she* doesn't know about Rule #1, either.

I wonder if you can show up at kindergarten wearing your baby shoes.

I'm sorry, baby shoe-wearers have to take rest time in the sub-basement. Good luck.

Okay. Back to my bedroom for more practice.

Loop, pull around, poke...

and pull.

MEEOOW!

Dad is so nice. He even bought me new laces.
That should help.

Snack time for Puddy.

LATER THAT DAY...

I know, I know—repeat after me: Shoelaces are <u>not</u> food.

My parents are taking me out for my favorite dinner—spaghetti—to celebrate the start of school. I don't see anything to celebrate.

Dad says, "Don't worry, sweetie. It just takes time." But kindergarten starts in two days! What if I have to wear a sign that says…

ONE DAY BEFORE KINDERGARTEN!

FIRST DAY OF KINDERGARTEN.

LATER THAT MORNING...

Really? Your dad tied your shoes for you? Me, too!

You guys can't tie your shoes, either?

You only know three kindergartners who can tie their shoes? Three, two, one? That's all?

I thought I was the only one.

I guess I'm not in such big trouble after all.